Rinsing
The Grapes

Ali & Anna Cohen

authorHOUSE®

AuthorHouse™ UK Ltd.
500 Avebury Boulevard
Central Milton Keynes, MK9 2BE
www.authorhouse.co.uk
Phone: 08001974150

First published by AuthorHouse 12/13/2011

ISBN: 978-1-4670-0339-1 (sc)
ISBN: 978-1-4670-0359-9 (e)

To Richard Leakey

I

The trouble with Boy started when he was just a baby, two and a quarter million years ago. Mum, the tribe's poet, was suckling him and singing out sunset, high in the forest canopy.

Darkness rose like a silent flood, bearing away every one of the familiar shapes. Only fireflies, dodging in and out of existence, some luminous toadstools on a rotten bough and her next companion, could be seen.

Mum's song involved repetitive chattering, ululation and shrieks of terror at night's power. As its rhythm took hold, the people began to stamp and sway. Some clapped their hands in time. A recognisable chorus appeared; they all joined each refrain in a medley of yells and screams. The sturdy branch swayed in counter-rhythm, shaking off old leaves.

Gradually the song built up, till at its climax, unable to contain herself, Mum took a great jump, emitting a last defiant squeal. Her foothold shifted while she was airborne, so she skidded and grabbed her neighbour with both hands. This saved her, but Boy's teeth had not yet erupted and his grip was feeble. With a smack his lips came free from her nipple. He fell.

The sensation of weightlessness was pleasant, but brief. His drowsy body crashed through a net of creepers with a waking yell and tumbled on. He landed in the feathery crown of a bamboo tuft so overgrown with liana and vine that it broke his fall four metres from the ground. He hung there by his armpits, swaying and bouncing. Mum's scream of loss was reciprocated by his own howls of pain and fear. They continued to address each other as she climbed down to get him, feeling her way from invisible hold to hold.

Boy became aware of many cuts and bruises; his arms felt dislocated; his cries redoubled. This attracted the attention of a leopard. Ready to eat, she had been planning the stalk of a particularly dangerous boar, his sow and their litter. She purred at the alternative. Man kittens were just the right size for a single meal and lacked sharp tusks. Larger game tended to get too high for pleasant eating before it could be finished. She hated waste.

She stole through the thicket until she could make out Boy's outline. She lunged at his hindquarters, but was baffled by the tangle of vines. She growled and leaned against the nearest stem. It bent obligingly, lowering Boy, but also herself. She tried to turn and pounce in one movement, but the released bamboo sprang back and a sharp leaf grazed her ear.

Boy was gibbering with terror by now and struggled like a sparrow in a cobweb. Bladder and bowels took on lives of their own. The leopard received a spattering in both eyes and worse, all over her nose. She snorted and slunk away as fast as the crowded stems allowed. The old boar's offspring were preferable after all. What a life, she grumbled, cleaning her muzzle on a tuft of grass; there was no such thing as a free meal!

Mum recovered Boy without further accident. The episode, "Dunging the Leopard" took its place in the saga of the tribe, chanted every full moon by senior males. Boy was honoured over all other children for his exploit, and received many a food-gift and grooming from even the most senior. But the damage was done. He never again felt safe in trees. He would cling, moaning, to a trunk, crying out every time it shifted in the breeze. He had to trust Mum, fingers in her hair, feet knotted on her back, as she swung and leaped to the food trees, but he insisted on being placed in the securest crook while she foraged far above.

II

As Boy grew he showed no sign of improvement. The giddy whirls of butterflies, vivid fowl darting through the void, shafts of sunlight obliquely penetrating the shifting foliage, vertical downpours hurtling past his perch, all filled him with terror. He would press his face against the reassuring bark, or cling to Mum blubbering inarticulately.

At first she put it down to a phase. She could remember being afraid of heights herself; it was odd to recall now she was in her prime, but a healthy respect for possible danger was the root of wisdom. Thanks to it she could now outclimb and outjump most of her rivals. She prided herself on being the best mother in the tribe. She always obtained the ripest fruit from the furthest extremities for her children.

Eventually she got irritable and even smacked him. It made her feel better, but no difference to him. And he was growing too heavy to be lugged around the treetops; even with the help of her sister, she felt unsafe. He was already tall and promised to be the lankiest of the tribe. This was a serious shortcoming for forest life. Also his feet were distorted, a web of skin extending far up his toes, so that their grip was lost. She had visions of a long fall, the three of them tripped by his clutch on some bough. The thought of the forest floor and its denizens, ready to pounce on their mangled remains, filled her with a dread equal to Boy's.

By the time he was seven he was badly undernourished, his transient celebrity long gone. Mum's milk was devoted to Baby, her gatherings to Middle Boy. He had to subsist on what was rejected, often on half-chewed husks. She was really worried by this apathetic wreck, without the respect of his peers and elders, and bullied even by the smallest toddler. So she gathered ripe avocados, guavas and a superb mango, arranged them in a weaver bird's nest and, with these offerings sought out the maturest and wisest of the tribe. He was in his usual place, resting his back against the bole, his bottom protected from the hard bark of the bough by a cushion of leaves.

"Hello, my dear niece and what can I do for you?" Wise Man could hardly be unaware of Boy, as they shared the same roost, but he felt his seniority and wide experience allowed a certain latitude. Why, he was so old that his head hair was falling out and some of the remainder was going white. He would be nineteen next year.

Mum handed over her gifts with the ritual obeisance. He greedily tore the parcel open and devoured its contents. She outlined her problems with Boy, hunkered respectfully, her hands and face on his feet. "Mmmm, not bad!" he muttered indistinctly, his eyes running down her shapely back. He reached to her rear to check if she was ripe. She shifted uneasily, wishing he would keep to the point and moved round to groom his hair. He settled, for the moment, soothed by the delightful tickling.

All Boy's symptoms were considered. Wise Man gave his preliminary opinion that this was just a phase. Mum dismissed it with a gesture, tweaking a sticky tuft of hair. "Careful" he said irritably, "That hurt. Well, this is a pretty little problem. I shall have to give it some thought. At the moment I regret that your delightful company is diverting my mind in quite a different direction. Perhaps it would be helpful if we relieved our tensions with a brief spell of copulation. Over the years I have found this a most useful aid to meditation, second only to sleep. When the latter succeeds the former, the result is almost invariably satisfactory. In addition, this course of action may lead to increase of the tribe."

"Over my dead body!" Dad barked from the other side of the tree, where he had been quietly listening to the interview. "She's mine and nobody else, least of all an old wreck like you, is going to interfere with her!"

Wise Man's hair stood on end in terror. "Am I to have no privacy for consultations?" he asked, submission in every syllable, "How can I be expected to deal with personal problems without confidentiality?"

"You can be as confidential as you like, if I exile you! Would you prefer to advise the kindly tiger, or the thoughtful python?" Dad's face, working with possessive rage, appeared round the bole. Wise Man made his formal bow and skipped to a lower branch, chattering with fear. Dad turned his attention to Mum, crouched against the trunk. He could smell she had come into season. No wonder she was so skittish; typical woman! But she laid into him before he could seize her.

"You are the end! You know how worried I am - about your eldest son. Wise Man is my last hope. You've been useless, but he might have a cure. But then you won't let me get on with it in peace. Oh no. You come and interrupt. Just when he was beginning to help too. I was only flirting; surely a little tease would be worth it. But no, you have to poke your great nose in! It's not my fault I have cycles. If you can't protect me from a creep like Wise Man, so much the worse for you. Men! They're so stupid! And the bigger, the stupider!"

Dad, fully upright, an imposing sight, advanced furiously, batting the words away from his ears as if they were flies. She could talk all right, but he'd teach her a lesson! She clambered swiftly round the tree and along a bough, well out of reach. Dad sat down as if to rest, blocking her return. Things weren't that urgent. She would be in season for a week. He could wait until they were ready to move off for the next meal.

After a while he grew impatient; he needed a bit of fun. Mum had chosen an isolated limb, and he made his way onto it. The branch bent under the load and Mum's grip tightened. She looked round for escape, but could see none. Dad grinned, took hold and began rocking. The branch waved in an increasing arc, carrying Mum with it. First she swore, then as he went on, she began to scream. The bough added a burden to her cries, groaning as if its heart was breaking. Finally Mum cracked and ran back so fast that she had half-climbed over his back before he seized her with a painful nip. She whimpered and submitted.

"Now let that be a lesson to you!" Satisfied by exercising power and by fertilising her, Dad released his downcast mate. The tribe settled for a peaceful snooze in the heat of the day.

III

Afternoon found the tribe gathered in a tree at the edge of the forest, beyond which grass was all that could could make a living out of the thin soil. This was no man's land, overlapping the territory of a troop of baboons. They did not take kindly to the intrusion. There was much yelling, and even throwing of sticks and stones. Then, waving a broken branch, with his bodyguard of semi-mature males, Dad drove them away. A straggler was knocked over and torn to pieces. The victors returned with the loot. As senior wife, Mum received a leg.

Boy cautiously licked it and exclaimed in pleasure at the salty taste. He seized the joint with both hands and bit deeply. The sinewy flesh was reluctant to part. He struggled with growing rage; at last a long shred snapped with such vigour that he tumbled backwards off the branch. He landed in a heap of leaves and dust, the meat a few yards off. He scuttled over and seized it, now coated with dirt. The next bite filled his mouth with grit. He spat and cursed. Mum joined him and examined the polluted meat, which had already attracted dozens of flies. She waved it in the air, narrowly missing a kite which had appeared from nowhere intent on scavenge. It squawked angrily and flapped over to a dead stump.

Mum returned to her bough with the meat. Middle Boy and she tried to clean it with their hands. It was no good. They dropped it. Boy rose on his hind legs. He had an unaccustomed sensation. He felt safe. Tentatively he tested a few falls. The ground did not hurt. He shouted with delight and ran in small circles round the tree. He jumped, he fell, he capered, he did the splits - it was a ballet! The tribe cheered him on. He had not been so happy for years. He picked up the leg and chucked it in the air. It flew past the tree top, scissoring open and shut, to splashd into a nearby pool, scaring numerous frogs which had been basking at its edge. In a volley of little splashes they buried themselves at the bottom.

Boy retrieved the dripping, hairy thing through a film of dusty scum. The delicious cool water on his arm enticed him to go further. He lay down, tried to breathe and surfaced in a coughing explosion. The disturbance terrified a frog out of its sense of self-preservation. It swam for land, passing between Boy's ankles. Without thinking he reached down and popped it in his mouth. One thrust of its hind legs, using his canine teeth for purchase, forced it to his uvula. He swallowed reflexively. With a slimy sensation in his mouth and an unquiet belly he felt the need of water. He took a long draught. Then he re-examined the joint; a tentative lick proved that the worst dirt had vanished. He settled in the pool to finish his meal. Soon nothing was left but the flail-like bones held by wiry sinews.

The tribe watched Boy from the safety of the tree. The baboon's remains had long since been consumed. A beer nut tree, the reason for their visit, had already been stripped by the rival troop. They were not only hungry but bored. It was extremely hot. Boy looked cool and comfortable sprawled in the pool. Like ripe fruit, the semi-mature males dropped to the ground with irregular thuds, followed at intervals by most of the rest of the tribe. Hesitantly, darting looks around, they rose on their hind legs and taking turns to lead, trailed each other to the pool. Boy opened a sleepy eye, recognised them and closed it.

Soon splashing and song resounded through the forest and diffused over the land. Wise Man observed that Boy seemed to have made an interesting innovation. He could not recall anyone staying on the ground so long and certainly nobody before had risked a snooze in the pool. Much annoyed by flies on his bloody face and forearms, Dad felt the attraction of a bathe and appointed Mum to watch for enemies. She settled in the highest crook of the tree with Baby, while he and Wise Man splashed into the water.

The view across the bare land, vibrating in the heat-haze, extended for some distance. It gradually rose to a low bluff, dissected by dry valleys. She could see little the other way, as the forest swiftly grew tall and dense. Nothing moved. Even the inert leaves had wilted. Her eyelids drooped. Dad relaxed in the soothing water and snored.

Wise Man was the first to move. Quietly he made his way to Mum, looking over his shoulder now and then, her appetising odour strengthening as he climbed. Mum had been far from pleased with Dad's morning game. He was strong, but brawn wasn't everything. A small act of revenge was due. Wise Man interested her. She was willing to trade. They mated.

Dad was roused by a frog burrowing under his neck. He leaped up with a shout of fear, turned and seized it.

A nice titbit, he reflected and methodically searched the shallows for more. Soon he had found a dozen. His juniors stood around the edge awaiting permission to join in. At last he reared up, a fat catch in hand and nodded; they splashed enthusiastically while he decided to take this gift to Mum. There she was, draped most unbecomingly along a branch half way down the tree, not at her post. He also noted Wise Man, casually leaning against the bole a yard or two below. They appeared to be deep in conversation; their postures radiated guilt.

He was not simple. Frog in hand, he lithely climbed up. He was right! Wise Man hunched as he passed, covering his loins, but, from this inappropriate source Mum's scent flooded his nostrils. As she leaned forward to receive the gift, he gave her a terrific slap. Baby nearly re-enacted Boy's fall, but she snatched him out of the air and leaped for her life to a lower bough. Dad was also an excellent kicker. His horny toes caught Wise Man in the throat, knocking him off the tree. His head struck a bough, and he lay still on the ground.

Mum reached a safe branch and from there began to abuse Dad, hair on end, cursing and screaming, beating her breast and ruefully massaging her numb ear. He replied in similar terms. The tribe gathered below, relishing Mum's imaginative turns of phrase and simile and the sheer strength and directness of Dad's utterance. Little murmurs of applause went up from time to time at the choicest epithets.

IV

All good things must come to an end. A resting pack of dogs had noted a commotion far below from a wash on the crest of the bluff. Later the smell of death reached their look-out. He signalled and they rose. They picked their way down the gully, invisible below its banks. Although it was not evening, they approached with all the caution of a proper hunt. They took their time, questing for scents, sterns waving jauntily.

The baboons were on a pile of rocks just beyond the valley. They were still lamenting their lost member, a vinegary old female, wise in the ways of snakes and scorpions and a leading authority on edible bulbs. "We will not see her like again" they moaned. The dogs passed by with the greatest care.

The pack proceeded to the point where the valley fanned out on the plain, a quarter of a mile from the pool. They slowed right down, their dun coats perfect camouflage among the boulders, dry grass and sand. They dodged from cover to cover and were still unobserved when they were within fifty yards.

Mum and Dad had shouted each other to a standstill, but it was not yet safe for her to make the appropriate approach to him. Wise Man roused, clutched his throat and stole away through the onlookers, to the pool. The frog, which had been dropped in the quarrel, hopped alongside, dust coating it with burning particles. They splashed into the soothing water. Bruised and scorched, but otherwise none the worse, the frog hid under a stone at the bottom.

Wise Man vigorously ducked, splashed face and throat and coughing, sucked up a great draught. As he rose and dashed water from his face, his eye caught a movement. A rock had grown legs and darted forward, then frozen back to stone. The whole expanse came to life, red-tongued mouths and hungry eyes closing at a gallop.

He did not wait to check. With a hoot of alarm he sprinted for cover. The tribe turned as one, took in the threat and scrambled in confused waves up the nearest trees. Boy was ten feet up a Pipal tree before its infinitesimal movements clutched his heart. He froze there, still holding the bones.

Wise Man arrived well before the pack. He scrambled up the easy handholds and was just reaching to swing onto the lowest branch when Dad's relentless fist caught him full in the mouth. He fell, spraining his ankle on a gnarled root. "Bugger off!" Dad ordered. *Revenge is sweet*, he thought, chuckling at Wise Man's dumbfounded, pleading face. His victim did not argue, but limped desperately for the next tree, the one occupied by Boy.

The pack had plenty of time to catch Wise Man. They stopped in a ring, those in front backing as he advanced, those behind nosing his heels. A half-grown puppy ran at him and tried to fasten on his buttock. He was saved by his irregular gait. The snap of teeth half an inch from his skin drove him into a despairing spurt. He jumped clumsily up the trunk and wrapped his legs round it. Swiftly he climbed, but the pack leader's jaws closed on his ankle. He screamed, continued to struggle upwards with his attacker and swarmed over Boy. His hand closed on the bone; thinking it was a branch, he pulled with all his weight. It slipped from Boy's grasp; by a frantic lunge Wise Man reached another hold as he toppled. The bone whistled with accidental precision into the bitch's eye. She opened her mouth to howl and tumbled to the ground.

This upset caused consternation. Never had the pack leader known such pain, not even when locked with a dog for days on end. Her followers had no idea what to do. Some lay down in the shade as she gambolled in agony, some crawled on their bellies to lick her, only to be snarled at and bitten. She rolled into the pool and its soothing touch restored her sanity. She rinsed the blood and humour off her muzzle and lay there, whining intermittently. Her pack's interest returned to the tribe and they settled round the occupied trees.

Dad and most of the tribe were hardly inconvenienced by the pack. They could return to the forest through the network of branches by which they had come. It was not so simple for Boy and Wise Man. From their tree the only route was over the ground. With the elder's injured leg a sprint was impossible. They would have to sit out the pack. It was sure to head for the uplands before nightfall, being at risk from both leopard and tiger if it stayed. These characters were fond of the spot and were wont to pounce on unsuspecting prey as it drank there. Wise Man was also well aware that his tree offered no refuge from such predators. He felt it was imperative to plan a retreat and to that end, opened negotiations with Dad.

The conversation did not go well. Dad was engaged in repeated congresses with Mum. His blood was up, she thought it wise to submit and he intended to erase the presumptuous seed. "Aargh! You treacherous old adulterer! Thus I wash you away, may your neck break in pieces, you bastard!" he ejaculated at the fourth climax. His eyes shifted to Boy's lanky frame. A new thought occurred to him. There was a distinct resemblance; they both had long narrow feet and their toes were unusually short, even before allowing for Boy's deformity. He bit Mum's ear furiously. "Bitch! Cheating on me from the first! That is no son of mine!" A weight of shame lifted from him.

Mum clapped a hand to her ear, disengaged, turned and seized his testicles with a shriek of rage. Wasting no words, she cupped them in one hand and punched with the other. He left the branch in a colossal leap and with considerable presence of mind, given the circumstances, seized a bough at his apogee.

He was disappointed to find that the branch was rotten and hardly detained him. He landed on the hindquarters of a large dog, breaking its back. His last thought before the pack preoccupied him, was pity for his successor, whoever he was; he'd have to cope with Mum. The unlucky frogs had the unusual experience of being consumed twice.

Before long Dad and the unfortunate dog were reduced to a scatter of cracked bones. The pack returned whence it came, led by the bitch, her head still held high, despite the pain in her blind eye. The patient kite swooped across from its perch, landed on Dad's upturned skull, whose thickness had defeated the pack's best efforts, and imbibed gratefully. It had a head start on the vultures which now arrived to clean up.

The tribe had watched the fall of its leader with horror and excitement. Deputy Dad felt nothing but elation. The first thing was to assert his authority. He therefore confirmed Dad's last curse, adding Boy to the sentence of exile. "May the tiger soon devour you!" he concluded, giving Mum a proprietorial nip. This was the recognised solemn oath by which the whole tribe was irrevocably bound. They joined in the execration, dusted their palms and turned their backs. With agile leaps they departed for the home range.

V

It was getting towards evening. Wise Man and Boy discussed the position for some time. They disagreed, Boy being very unwilling to follow the tribe, Wise Man's injury supporting this, but he still insisting that this was the safest option.

There was a commotion in the bushes a hundred yards away. An antelope bounded into the open, hotly pursued by an angry buffalo, which it had evidently disturbed as it browsed. Behind them, a disappointed growl sent both off in opposite directions along the fringe of the forest. They dived back at what they judged to be a safe distance and silence fell.

The jungle was full, the savannah empty. Without further discussion they set off uphill as fast as possible. Both were well-watered and fed. They could last at least a couple of days before they needed more. Wise Man used the baboon leg as a clumsy crutch. Boy blubbered as he went, missing Mum. He was shushed, not unkindly, by his elder.

Soon they reached the top of the bluff. The dogs had moved on up country and the land ahead was empty.

They looked back. The sun was on its way down behind the jungle. Boy thought he could hear the faint evening howls of the tribe, carried to him over gold-rimmed tree tops. It was a magnificent, if overblown, view. He sobbed miserably as they plodded over the brow. The tableland continued for perhaps half a mile to another bluff, this time much steeper. Parts were cliff. By the time they were near the sun had gone. A bright full moon in a clear sky replaced it. It revealed a group of hyaenas fresh from their day's rest in a cave at the bottom of the cliff.

Wise Man had seen stray hyaenas before and disliked them. There was something about their knowing abject expressions that reminded him of his own status in the tribe, but they had extraordinarily powerful jaws. When they appeared in force, eyes glowing in the moonlight, he nearly collapsed in terror. Boy forced him on the few yards to the cliff and, in the nick of time, up a narrow ledge which climbed the scarp.

Wise Man turned and swung his crutch at a particularly bold one which had followed. It neatly caught the bone in its mouth and leaped down with its prize. A whimpering scuffle broke out while they hurried on. They were soon high up, the ledge narrowing as they went. Boy was surprised that he felt no fear; solid rock was a different proposition to wood.

The hyaenas, having disposed of the bones, divided forces, a couple scampering up the ledge, the rest keeping pace along the ground. Boy and Wise Man arrived at an eroded fault in the cliff. Over the years it had weathered into a steep chimney, reaching at an acute angle nearly to the top. Nothing but a foothold remained of the ledge. With practiced ease they swung round the corner, but without hands their agile pursuers were baulked. With great caution, complaining and bickering, they backed down the way they had come. They rejoined their comrades and, after some debate, all made off after easier quarry far to the south.

Morning, cold and misty, a complete contrast to the equable forest, found the couple huddled together in the chimney, their stomachs growling. The hyaenas had not returned, having found a dead stegodon miles away. Wise Man became aware of an itching in his injured ankle. The scab of each tooth mark was puffed by pus which sprang forth as he scratched. The sweet smell of decay offended their nostrils. Wise Man was well acquainted with infections from biting flies and rodents. He searched among the rocks and soon had a poultice of moss which was applied to the wound and secured with a string of grass.

They scrambled up the chimney, cursing as sharp edges dug into their shins and kneecaps. Twenty feet below the rim of the summit, a weak stratum had been shattered so badly by frost and rain that chunks had dropped out, creating a shady hollow. They paused just below, listening intently for sounds of life. This sort of shelter was favoured by many predators. Nothing broke the silence. After a pause Boy lobbed a pebble into the opening. The effect was startling. With a grinding crash the whole back wall collapsed in a cloud of dust and poured over the lip. They crouched instinctively, clutching the chimney face. In a moment the avalanche had passed. They rose, eyes glaring from masks of ochre dust, gave identical screams of terror, then clutched each other and burst into laughter.

Boy lobbed a second pebble into the void. It rolled away hollowly, then, after a short pause, a faint splash came back. Wise Man gave a grunt of delight. He could hardly believe their luck. There were no other signs of life.

They cautiously hauled themselves into the cave. The stone had dislodged a pile of scree from an ancient rock fall. It had masked a deep recess that angled downwards into the earth. It would not be possible to see its depths until late afternoon, when the sun would shine directly into its mouth. In the meantime they took no risks, but sat at the edge, ready to dive off at the first sign of danger.

Boy began grooming Wise Man's dusty frame. The latter turned over to expose his other side and in so doing, became aware that a root laid across the bare rock beside him was oozing red sap from a scuffed patch of scales. "Scales!" His reaction was as rapid as a cat's. He was ten feet down the chimney before the thought completed itself: "Snake!" Boy matched his actions, unaware of their cause.

After chewing the matter over, Wise Man concluded that the snake was probably dead or paralysed by the rock fall. Boy volunteered to reconnoitre. With sloth-like care and a mongoose's alertness, he climbed to a vantage point by the cave and surveyed the beast. Its head was buried by a huge block of stone. A thin trickle of blood suggested that it was at least seriously injured. Its immobility argued for death.

This was sufficient to encourage Wise Man to return. With considerable trepidation, he pinched the limp tail, jumping away from any reaction, but there was none. They grew bolder. Boy picked up a heavy rock and smashed it down on the part nearest its buried end. There was no reaction and could be none after that.

It turned out to be a king cobra. Its meat was very palatable and their stomachs were soon full. A half-digested, pre-tenderised cane rat was a bonus, its belly full of fermenting sugar. An unwonted mood of levity took over. They laughed and tumbled about, as senseless as children. The sun stole over the lip of the cliff and flooded the platform.

"This beats that mouldering forest!" shouted Wise Man, exposing his wounded ankle to the sun's healing rays. "It's like the Happy Age before people were driven into the trees."

"All we need is women!" Boy replied in a terse, manly way.

The happy pair retreated from the burning sun and settled for a siesta against the shady wall, twitching and burping as their meal settled.

It was late afternoon when the sun touched them again. They stirred, yawned luxuriously, opened their eyes and sprang upright with cries of alarm. Memory returned and Wise Man calmed Boy, who had been frightened by his disorientation. He led the way into the cave. A deep cleft crossed the passage. They looked down and jumped back; two appalling masks had glared up at them. The cave was already inhabited!

Wise Man called out a quavering enquiry; the reply was a booming growl. They crept back to the cleft and as their eyes passed the lip, were matched by an equally cautious pair of heads peering up. A dislodged pebble broke the image into a jumble. Wise Man suppressed his consternation and explained the phenomenon to Boy, who needed no instruction, having often studied pools of water in the forks of the trees. He also knew about echoes and so, ignoring Wise Man's continued expatiation, ruefully enquired "Are we really that hideous?"

Wise Man did not reply; he was very thirsty and was descending to the water's edge. Boy scrambled down after him, lost his balance and splashed into the pool. He had never felt anything so cold! He gave a shrill scream as the water climbed above his thighs and continued up to his chin. His feet came to rest on jagged rocks covered in slime. He kicked for the bank and scrambled out, bleeding and numb. Wise Man cackled, hunkered down and delicately cupped his hands to raise the icy water to his mouth. He leaned forward. His foothold proved unstable and dropped him in the pool. It was no laughing matter, the water covered his head. Only with great difficulty did he struggle ashore, teeth chattering, swearing and moaning, a bedraggled wreck.

The westering sun passed the cave mouth, throwing an orange glare to the furthest end. The shivering pair found a ledge round the pool and explored as far as they could. The cave narrowed swiftly to a cleft too small to pass. There was no sign of animal life, apart from a few stray woodlice.

"This looks the safest spot to sleep tonight." Boy remarked. Wise Man would have liked to disagree, but its truth was too obvious, so he contented himself with grumbling about the distance they would have to carry their bedding. Thus reminded, they hurried out to collect armfuls of dry grass. The involuntary wash had removed most of the dust and their glossy brown skins glistened in the sunlight through their thin coats.

Till now they had been too busy to investigate the cliff-top. They scrambled up and found themselves on a grassy, well-cropped plateau, peopled, at some distance, by thousands of antelope and other grazing beasts. Thorny shrubs, festooned with vines and flowering creepers, were dotted about at random. Half a mile away an ancient and enormous fig tree sprawled in a haywire tangle. The honking of hornbills and clumsy crashes shaking its foliage, suggested that fruit was available. The plateau stretched away, apparently for ever, gradually losing definition until it shimmered into empty air.

The picture was completed by the sumptuous form of a leopard stretched on the sun-warmed edge of the cliff, three hundred yards from them. It opened its eyes lazily at Wise Man's yelp of terror, but having fed at dawn, was still more sleepy than hungry. It yawned, scanned the newcomers and closed its eyes again. Wise Man picked up a stout stick and, clutching this, set about gathering his bed. Boy followed suit, holding a heavy pebble. They soon had sufficient and returned.

"If we can get in and out, so can a leopard, or a tiger, or a bear!" Boy's worry was too well-founded for Wise Man to offer easy comfort. But as they relieved themselves at the edge, he did remark that their hole was at least as safe as any tree top.

The short-lived illumination went with the sun and they nestled together, chewing at ends of the snake's remains till their teeth clashed on the last morsel. Then they dropped off.

VI

Dawn came. The mist burnt off the uplands. Browsers moved to and fro in the irrational hope of finding verdant pastures untouched by their companions. As it was late in the dry season they were bound to be disappointed. Soon they would have to move further north to exploit the low-lying meadows which became available as the rivers dried out.

"Today does not feel too promising." Wise Man muttered when he finally woke. He massaged the small of his back with his knuckles and groaned as each vertebra shifted. "All this ground work is doing me a mischief. If the Creator had meant us to stay upright he wouldn't have given us hands to rest on." He hunkered down on the platform at the cave mouth and toyed idly with the sand and dust. He examined his wound, picked off the healthy scabs that had formed and licked the fresh blood that sprang forth, until the flow slackened and the tissue began to dry. He re-covered it with a poultice of moss. The rusty taste of blood brought saliva flooding into his mouth and his belly was speared by pangs of hunger.

Boy gave no sign of waking, let alone rising. His dark nest was so comfortable that he was still in the deepest of dreamless slumbers. Wise Man felt a growing irritation at the contrast between his uncomfortable alertness and Boy's idle drowsing. He picked up some gravel and hurled it at the rear of the cave. The action gave his elbow and shoulder a painful jar, while the missiles rattled and splashed into the pool. Boy slept on.

He admitted defeat, clambered back on his feet and returned to the nest. He shook the boy by the hair until he woke with a groan. "What's the matter?" were his first words, then "Where's the food? I could eat a giant sloth!"

Wise Man indicated the cave mouth as a first step towards breakfast. He felt his own depression lift as Boy voiced his hunger and annoyance at being woken. They climbed into the cleft and drank from its chilly reservoir. Boy was cuffed for starting to urinate. "First rule: Never piss in your drink, or shit in your bedding. Didn't Mum teach you anything?"

Of course Boy had been thoroughly trained, but the application of forest rules to their changed situation took some working out.

They came to the cave mouth and studied the land below. Nothing moved but tufts of burnt brown grass and desiccated bushes, dancing in the heat. Any predators would have to be in dire need to be willing to move out of whatever shade they had found. They stood there for some time, enjoying the view, until Boy had finished.

Wise Man spoke up. "It occurs to me that the heat of the day is the safest time to look for food. There's nothing below. What do you say to exploration of the land above? That fig tree looked promising, though I expect those birds have already helped themselves to the choicest fruit. Let's hope the leopard has gone."

Boy eagerly agreed, his stomach growling. "Well, off you go then," Wise Man ordered, sitting down with a grunt of satisfaction, "Don't forget to fetch enough for our evening meal and tomorrow's breakfast as well."

Boy was not having this. He stood where he was. "Not likely." he growled, his voice taking on what would have been a menacing note had it been an octave deeper. "What I do, you do; where you go, I go."

"The word you are seeking is probably 'together'!" Wise Man suggested in his most pedantic tone. "I would quite agree with you, but unfortunately my leg is still poorly and in my opinion, needs at least another week's rest. And that ducking yesterday has given me rheumatism and a nasty cough." He hacked out a few unconvincing gasps, rubbing his back.

Boy was already irritable and saw this wheedling for what it was, an ineffectual attempt to gain ascendancy. He snatched off the bandage and sniffed the reddened area. He knew a sound and healthy scar as well as the next man. He gave Wise Man a contemptuous kick and his first order. "Come."

With further grumblings and exaggerated favour to his weakened limb, Wise Man hauled himself up, making as if to lean on Boy. The latter pushed him away and received a nasty bite on the heel of his palm. It bruised the flesh, but did not break the horny skin. With honours, even the companions started for the top of the cliff.

The sun struck their faces like a flame as they pushed above the overhang. Once their eyes had adjusted to the glare they could see the grassland stretching away, cropped to the root, with not a beast in sight. The fig tree was the only relief in the whole landscape. They hurried towards it, anxiously darting looks around as they went, to find that the plateau, far from being a plain, was cut at irregular intervals by steep-sided dry gullies. Their sense of danger mounted to fever pitch as they crossed them.

They were pouring sweat by the third descent and awkward scramble up the far side and by the fifth, were as thirsty as if unwatered for two days. They were therefore greatly relieved to clamber out of the last, dash across the final sun-baked expanse and collapse in the blessed shade. Some hornbills threw themselves out of the boughs with angry cries and flapped off towards the forest, which, for them, was only a minute or two away.

Once their heartbeats and breaths had slackened, the thought of ripe juicy fruit recurred. Wise Man prospected through the twisted members as high as he could go and soon was cramming his mouth with pink-hearted, succulent fruit. Boy foraged below and was rewarded with dozens of pecked figs which had been knocked down by the birds. Then he came across clusters of ripe grapes dangling from the vines that rambled in and out of the boughs. He pushed a bunch into his mouth. Juice spurted. It was ecstasy!

He stepped forward through thigh high undergrowth to reach the next bunch and lost his footing. He fell with a shout down a steep slope onto a soggy pad of vegetation that swayed and sank beneath him. The fig's branches concealed the spot completely from above. He stood up; his feet sank straight through into soft mud. Flailing his arms desperately he fell backwards and sank below the yielding watery mat. From past experience he was aware that it was not possible to breathe under water, so pushed his face back above the surface. The mud gently clung to his hands and as he freed them, his face sank back below the surface. The struggle continued for some time, but at length he sat upright in the morass, which only reached half way up his chest.

Wise Man observed his efforts from a neighbouring bough and made encouraging and helpful comments: "Try to stand up; no, try to turn round; no, stay there; I'll come and lend you a hand." Slowly he began to descend.

Boy found his legs were free and swiftly pushed himself on his backside to the edge, where he seized a bough and clambered out, dripping mud and stinking horribly. Wise Man noted his escape and returned to foraging.

Boy found that the pool extended for only a few yards and was bounded on three sides by a sheer wall of rock. It was more a silted sink hole than a pool. The undergrowth was so dense on the one sloping bank and the rest were so steep, that it was inaccessible to most animals. It lay there vacant and secret, occasionally trapping and drowning unwary beasts that blundered into it. In the rainy season it would fill to the brim, then gradually fall to its muddy base as the ground dried out.

"I name this The Water Hole." Wise Man and Boy, full-bellied, sprawled beside it.

"Mud Hole would be better!" Boy replied, picking dried flakes from his thighs. A crazed film of silt had formed on the lower two thirds of his body.

"I have spoken: So shall it be."

Boy found a damp lump of mud in his crotch, scraped it out and rolled it thoughtfully into a ball.

"Wise Man?"

"Yes?"

"You know what Dad said, just before he fell."

"Yes."

"Was he right? Is it true? Are you really my father?"

He darted a shifty look at Boy, whose candid glance met his. *He'll be lying, whatever he says next,* Boy thought. He flicked the mud ball back in the pool.

Wise Man took a little time, making up his mind which reply was most advantageous. He plumped for the immediate status fatherhood would confer. A flicker of imagination showed Boy waiting upon him with armfuls of food, kowtowing respectfully, even finding him a mate and handing her over.

"It saddens me to have to admit such a sin, but yes, you are indeed the unhappy result of a brief and intense affair between my wretched self and Mum. Love overcame prudence. Dad's tyranny made secrecy vital... Could you fetch a bunch of grapes; I think I have enough room for them."

"Fetch them yourself." Boy replied without heat.

"As your father, surely you will agree that I am entitled to proper respect and service. It would otherwise be a very poor precedent for the conduct of your own children to you."

"Bollocks! I'm sure to have hundreds of children out here miles from the tribe! Are you proposing to be their mother, father? It's your fault too!" The future prospects had not occurred to him before and he fell silent.

"My dear child, when you are older you will understand the dire necessity that drives a man to take appalling risks when a woman is in season! In any case it is useless to chew over the unchangeable past. We must make the best, that's the spirit. Our position is not bad. We have food in abundance, secure water supplies and shelter." He had raised himself on an elbow in the energy of talk. Now he slumped back, smiled complacently and closed his eyes.

Boy rose quietly, feeling queasy from this dose of wisdom. He made as if to groom the elder and the latter

29

relaxed into receptive pose. He was near the edge of the water hole. The next moment he was rolling and sank into the weeds with a curse and muffled splash.

"You need to wash your mouth, father!" Boy shouted at the indignant head which surfaced under a vivid wig of algae.

"It comes to something when your own son does a thing like that to you!" Wise Man observed, as he agilely mounted the slope.

"Father! Kiss my arse!" Boy moved behind a bed of nettles and tangled creepers, well out of reach and, as a precaution, picked up a thick, broken branch. Wise Man settled down, biding his time, and became preoccupied scraping slime and weeds from head and body.

VII

The sun had passed its third quarter when the pair, forgetting their differences, began to forage for supper. They soon had a mound of succulent figs and grapes, the latter on a coil of vine knawed off at both ends. The resident nests of ants scented an unheard-of accumulation of food, and marshalled their workers. They poured from crevice and hole in nervous lively swarms and would soon have submerged the stocks had Wise Man not noticed and briskly removed them to a safer spot in the shallow water. He left an overripe fig, its orifice weeping juice, to distract them. Fighting soon broke out over this and preoccupied the scavengers.

Boy wondered aloud whether it would not be safer to stay put overnight rather than risk the trek back, encumbered with stores. Wise Man's nape bristled with fear at the prospect of such a spot after dark. He listed the vast concourse of enemies, some of which were as capable as he, let alone Boy, of climbing.

The latter interrupted him with exasperation - "No, I didn't mean that, but what about the edge of the water hole. It's so well-hidden that it could only be found by accident and look what happened to me! The stink from the mud must cover our scent."

"So we're to become bog dwellers are we? What if something does find us? I suppose we jump into the mud up to our necks! No thanks; I don't want to become a giant frog!"

"I don't see ..." Boy was responding irritably, when a thump and crash from the other side of the grove froze him with open mouth. They moved together silently and backed towards the water. Boy gripped his branch with both hands and pointed it at the sounds which seemed to be approaching. Wise Man picked up a jagged rock. The pit took on the appearance of a trap. Boy now agreed with Wise Man's view. They looked round wildly and crawled back up the slope in order to skirt its far side.

They were half way round, when something huge and dark briefly crashed into sight between dangling foliage, and disappeared. It gave a loud snort and heavy cough, reappeared, then lumbered down the little slope to the water's edge. It dwarfed the pile of fruit which had evidently attracted it. It stooped and, opening its huge mouth, engulfed a quarter of the fodder. It emitted a strange call which was promptly responded to by a guttural fluting cry and a similar beast, only half its size, joined it. This was evidently a female, judging by the double row of full-teated breasts on its front. Boy studied the newcomers with interested terror; he had never seen or heard of such monsters.

The giant, a male, was like a caricature of Dad; its long cranium, thickly clothed with coarse hair, was set low over deep-set hollows, within which only the distant glint of eyes could be made out. Its body was covered with a thick black coat and where skin was visible, this too was purplish black. Its back was bent in a permanent bow and its left knuckle hung comfortably at the same level as its feet. The right arm was extraordinarily long, its further half ending in a nodular lump. The massive thighs and shins were almost as short as they were broad in their splay. The female was built on a much lighter scale, with a finer pelt and a face all but bald; there was only a faint trace of hair along the jaw line and around the lips.

The male discarded its limb extension. For a weird moment Boy thought it was disjointing itself. Then he realised it had been carrying a small tree trunk with its root ball. This sign of power was equally disturbing, but in a more understandable way. It scooped up another quarter of the fruit and with surprising delicacy, offered it to its companion. The face fell apart, disclosing two rows of massive white teeth. One would have filled Boy's mouth. She accepted the gift with much chatter and gesticulation. Her hands were as eloquent as her mouth; she had the same number of digits as Boy. She picked the fruit one by one from his palm with her mobile lips. Only when she had emptied it and sat back, did the male toss the rest of the fruit to the back of his mouth in a single scoop.

They hunched down on all fours and lowered their mouths to the water, which they filtered by the simple expedient of pressing the mat of vegetation below the surface. Their consumption was such that the level fell visibly as they drank. The female rose first and as she did, her eyes met Boy's. She tugged the hairy arm of her companion and giggled. He was still drinking and failed to react immediately.

Boy did not stay. He ran for his life, crashing through the shrubs, ducking his head to avoid low branches and was almost instantly in the open. His headlong rush sent Wise Man, who had been standing there, sprawling.

A leopard had been confronting the solitary figure. It grunted in surprise at the sudden arrival and twitched its tail irritably as it considered the new situation. The stick brandished in front of Boy looked as if it could hurt; on the other hand he looked a far superior specimen to his stringy companion. Mind made up, it crouched for a decisive pounce, only to be distracted by another series of crashes in the undergrowth.

The strangers stepped out a few yards away. The leopard spat and shifted its hindquarters to take in this new threat. The giant rose to his full height and calmly considered his opponent. The cat crouched lower, glaring. After a minute's confrontation, it was the leopard whose eyes shifted. With a sideways bound it was in the foliage.

Boy had lost all fear of his saviours and rushed to them in gratitude. Wise Man followed with some misgivings. The huge figure turned and extended its sinewy hand. It held Boy firmly by the shoulder, removed his stick and then examined him carefully, a look of bewildered delight on its face. The female also clasped him and went over his whole body touching and sniffing. Boy became aware of their characteristic scent, a sharp and poignant odour, vaguely reminiscent of peccary, but with an underlying roundness which was not unlike the tribal perfume. His head was pushed into the male armpit and vigorously rubbed; a moment later Wise Man received the same treatment. They were released and stood in an incongruous group, grinning uncertainly.

"Well, what now?" Wise Man's anxiety grew as the shadows lengthened. "Should we get back to the cave? That leopard will not be a good companion if we stay here. On the other hand, I don't want to show the cave to these two. They might kick us out, or eat us!"

No further thought was needed. The male took Wise Man's wrist, the female Boy's and set off across the upland away from the cave. Wise Man's protests were as ineffective as his attempts to free himself. He felt as helpless as if he was hanging by the arm from some cleft in a bough, waiting for ants to eat him alive.

The female held Boy less firmly, as they were better matched in size, but he made no protests, happy to be with such strong protectors. Also, as he became accustomed to it, her bouquet began to intrigue him. There was an element which was faintly reminiscent of Mum, yet the total effect was excitingly different. It had sexiness about it. He began to feel the same influence that he had seen reduce the ineligible males of his tribe to abject wrecks; they would wander round for days on end, weak with hunger, unable to concentrate, feed, or obtain relief, their staring coats riddled with parasites, until the cycle of fertility was over. She seemed unaware of her effect and cuddled, kissed and nuzzled him as they went.

It occurred to Wise Man that perhaps they had been mistaken for young relatives, so qualifying for adoption. In fact he saw that there were resemblances between them, though he felt the differences in build and adaptation were enough to make them only distant cousins. All the same, he felt more kinship with them than with the tribes of monkeys which so often annoyed the tribe in the forest, or with baboons. They went on at a rapid clip as darkness fell.

They continued far into the night. Wise Man and Boy were shattered by the time the group halted for a rest in one of the gullies. The giant used the narrow end of his club to excavate a hole in the bed which soon filled with a shallow puddle. Then he pushed handfuls of grass in to filter the water. They all drank deeply from the resulting fluid, which still had a salt earthy flavour and encouraged them to drink more than they really needed. Then they went on steadily towards the source of the sun.

The land changed. They loped beside a huge gorge whose far side could only faintly be made out in the glimmering darkness. A rock face reared ahead. The giant knew his way and led them for half a mile through a cleft which snaked between sheer walls. They debouched in an amphitheatre whose open side was the edge of the gorge, while cliffs beetled above from all other angles. The ground had a strong dip, due to an age-old accumulation of scree from the cliffs.

Wise Man and Boy were released. They lay down on the ground, just as they were and were asleep in moments, their escorts studying them with deep attention, as they blissfully snored and whistled.

VIII

While the exiles were engaged in this way, the tribe experienced considerable vicissitudes. Deputy Dad, or 'Father' as he entitled himself, despite his lack of issue, lacked Dad's long experience and instinct for security. The tribe moved its roost, the old one holding unsuitable memories, to a huge mahogany half a mile away. It was very old and hollow. The opening between its massive roots was concealed by thick greenery.

This cavity housed a giant python, one of the last of its kind. Its problems had compounded as it aged, for there was no upper limit to its growth and its need for food increased in proportion to its decreasing mobility. It was in a perpetual state of starvation. So with great pleasure it noted the vibration from songs and quarrels overhead as the tribe settled. It made a formidable sight, exuding its hundred foot length and corkscrewing up the trunk. Its tongue sensed substantial victuals, whose presence grew stronger as it climbed. If it had not been so malnourished it would have slithered upon its prey without warning.

Father had made the cardinal error of choosing for his roost a broad bough from which there was no retreat.

He felt splendid isolation would enhance his prestige. It floated far above the forest floor, creating a little clearing by its shade. The rest of the tribe were further up, in the crown.

The python slumped clumsily upon Father's bough and advanced its questing head. He could only scream in terror and withdraw until he was swaying among the remotest creaking foliage. His pursuer had to extend its whole length along the branch before it could wrap him up. It anchored halfway out and, with deliberation, reeled him in, his hands clutching twigs and scrabbling at bark, as if they could help. As he was lofted for crushing, he writhed and struggled, hoping to slip free on his sweat. This was enough for the snake to lose its balance and flop under the branch. It halted with a mighty jerk on its knotted tail, but only momentarily, as the bough snapped. The tree could not cope with such stress.

Father, python and branch landed with a terminal crash. He died instantly and the python, its body a mass of breakages, soon followed. Nothing was wasted. They nourished a tiger and her half-grown cubs for as long as it took to eat from nose to tail-tip.

The tribe was leaderless for the second time in as many days. The remaining seniors had equal right to the vacant position, as Father had not had time to choose and nominate a loyal henchman. First thing next morning, a series of fights broke out between the rivals, during which two died. Half a dozen were left glowering at each other from separate branches, cut, bitten and bruised. Mum and the other females, with the semi-senior and other immature males, ensconced in a nearby tree, placidly chewing, showed no disposition to favour any one contender. It was a stand-off, and without Wise Man's guidance nobody knew what to do. A truce was patched up to allow everyone to feed and roost.

A period of anarchy followed. Groups dispersed to separate parts of the ancestral territory, creating an irregular patchwork of miniature ranges. None went beyond the outer limits as this would have amounted to exile. They hung on, each guarding his plot, hoping to attract enough support to take over. Many fell victim to predators, malnutrition and disease and numbers dropped to an unheard-of level. At last the survivors coalesced into a single tribe comprising three mature males, seven females and assorted children of various ages.

Mum came into season again. The rivalry of her three would-be mates took an even more bitter edge. Many a bruise and scratch was inflicted. But she refused to get involved. Soon afterwards the lesser females all came on heat and the stress was relieved. It was still felt that whoever Mum condescended to favour would become the new leader, and the three still pressed her.

She was still undecided and happily enjoying her status, when events took a new turn.

The other females were much smaller than she and although they coveted her place, any one was unable to mount a serious challenge. At a given moment, the whole group set upon her. The jungle again rang with screams of pain and cries of anger and predators pricked up their ears. The sounds of conflict moved towards the wide river bounding the tribal land. Mum was retreating with the tribe in hot pursuit. Middle Boy and Baby were her only companions.

Evening found the losers crouched miserably in an isolated tree on a river spit. The rest of the tribe took up station in the next tree, some way off, jeering and throwing sticks. It had been a tricky fifty-yard dash. They had only just beaten the sleepy crocodiles. It took them a few vital seconds to register the presence of food and dart forward. They grunted angrily as their hurtling bodies collided. After baring their teeth to each other, they crawled dejectedly back to their muddy quarters.

Night fell, the tribe went off to roost and Mum sank in deep thought. The position seemed hopeless. It was only a matter of time before some leopard came sniffing round. The jungle was hostile and the river barred retreat. She gave in and sobbed, as the moon rose, hugging her children.

Far off in the mountains two days before, a violent cloudburst fell. A turbulent flood rushed down, ripping new paths in the soft valley, drowning its denizens, tearing loose huge trees, roots and all and hurling them along its course. In a narrow gorge a particularly massive hulk dammed the flow and, with debris trapped against it, built up a powerful head of water.

At length the pressure was too great. The timber gave and a wall of water broke away with a roar. The chafing jumble settled as it entered the lower reaches. It flowed on, smooth and powerful, pocked with debris, towards the distant lake where it would die among barren salt flats. Along its course the water level silently rose. The floating tree went on, rolling and hesitating as it caught on the river bed and then jerking back, as it righted itself.

Mum was woken at dawn by Middle Boy's hiss of surprise. The stray tree had snagged on the roots of their refuge, swung round and halted beside it. He scrambled onto it and without thought she followed with Baby. Among the dangling weeds and broken foliage a harvest of bedraggled nuts still hung. Cheerfully they foraged and soon sat back, their bellies full, with plenty left for consumption once the first intake had settled. They were safe from the attacks of everything except pythons, the dangerous bank being well out of reach. Mum rested in a daze of digestion, thankful at their good luck, and passively watched the treetops as they slipped past.

With a thrill of terror she realised the trees were not moving - she was! She spun round. Their roost was just vanishing round a bend. They had broken free with unfelt gentleness and were adrift on the wide river.

They finished the nuts the first day. Luckily the water was too deep for submerged branches to snag the bottom and roll them in during the night. A drowned jungle swine became entangled in the roots. They fished it out and dined on its tender rank flesh, which fell apart as they tore it. They endured upset stomachs for the rest of that day and night.

The third morning, the forest thinned out and retreated from the banks. The river entered a wide canyon, its course interrupted at intervals by step-like rapids. They poured smoothly over the first, the family clambering up and down like agile hyraxes as they rolled.

The next fall was broad and shallow and they ran upon rocks. The tree swung round with a terrible grinding and its roots crashed into the bank. Mum could take a hint. They dashed along the trunk and leaped upon dry land. They mounted a jumble of boulders at top speed, found a hollow at the top of a huge monolith and collapsed. They were hidden, except from the distant top of the gorge and only if scented were they in danger. They slept.

As far as the rest of the tribe is concerned, an able leader emerged, order was restored and numbers returned to normal. Several lived to a ripe old age, though none quite achieved Wise Man's record. Generations later a great drought destroyed forest and tribe.

IX

Wise Man christened his new protectors Big and Little. Their language was far more eloquent than the tribe's. It consisted of infinite combinations of hoots, grunts, giggles, voiced and unvoiced consonants, thirteen distinct tones, clicks, howls, gestures and scent. Every utterance was governed by a strict sequence of multi-layered rhythms and counter-rhymes. He threw up his hands in despair when he learnt enough for its insuperable difficulties to become obvious. Boy made more progress, but his armpit was not versatile enough. It would not produce the right secretion to preface each discourse with the required honorific odour. Nor could he produce the mandatory simultaneous double-toned click and hoot after each third phrase. Each time he spoke, it was an insult, to the amusement of his instructors.

Fortunately Big and Little soon picked up the tribal tongue, to them a childish patois. After a few days of routine, feeding, driving away predators and finding night shelter, they also learned most of the vocabulary. Its simplicity and lack of expressiveness continually amazed them. They were stunned to discover there was only one word for water. The difficulties, the misunderstandings, the danger this could cause! They doubled up in fits of laughter as they enacted some of the possible contretemps.

Wise Man was unamused. "I'd like to see you nipping through the treetops like us! You wouldn't look so clever splattered on the ground like burst melons. Come to think of it, that might be an improvement, you're so ugly, you great hairy brutes."

This was received with good humour. Big's only comment was a loud fart. Thanks to his wholesome diet of herbs and roots, the effect was not too terrible. It was sufficient for the group to move off from the draughtless hollow where they had been resting.

One of the tasks of the ground dwellers was to burn off the dead grass at the end of each dry season.

Long ago lightning had ignited a dry stump on the edge of a scarp. The tinder-like bole flared off in an ardent glow. Its roots smoked for weeks and eventually lit a layer of peat in which they were embedded. This in its turn smouldered covertly until it reached the face of the scarp and spread along the whole exposed stratum. It burnt for months.

One of Big's ancestors had noted that the forage next season after a fire was sweeter and tenderer than usual and had fewer unpleasant pests. He decided to experiment. Seizing a tuft of grass, he lit it from the peat fire and carried the blazing torch to the nearest area of hay. A pall soon darkened the sky and flames spluttered through the tangled golden stems. Terrified game fled, leaving behind smoking carcasses of the slow and infirm. As expected, next season's crop was most satisfactory and he grew fat.

The following dry season the peat fire died out. Years of idleness now paid off. A regular pastime of the ground dwellers during the long dull evenings was to hold debates, arm-wrestling contests and other entertainments. Once they had considered the deeper problems of existence, which were solved by a sustained chord of all possible tones and odours, held for ten heartbeats of earsplitting sound, they moved to lighter matters. Among these were competitions to produce the best and most decorative showers of sparks. The custom had developed from a more primitive rock-throwing event.

The ancestor concerned was a three years' champion. He had obtained his best results, not by hurling a flint against the rock wall in the traditional way, but by banging two together. With this technique he had defeated five visiting teams, despite their appeals to the referee. The decision had gone against them, as there was no real difference between concussion against a rock in a cliff and one in hand. He recalled the painful scorches he sometimes received in the heat of contest. Perhaps sparks could make fire. He tested this by igniting the leaf litter furnishing his riverside cave. The method worked. It was uninhabitable for weeks, stinking of smoke and coated in soot. So the savannah could be polluted again and he could confidently expect fresh food.

The tradition was handed down and Big's people would soon have become as numerous as the sands, had not other browsers taken advantage of the improved grazing. They invaded in irresistible herds, making life even more chancy than before. For with them came dangerous predators which had only rarely been encountered in earlier days.

To Wise Man fire was a nightmare. Fortunately the forest was too moist to burn freely, but he had seen the effects of lightning upon an unlucky relative. He had smelt terror in the smoke drifting down from the dry uplands. He had seen scorched animals limping through the forest, driven from their homes by fire. So he was shocked to see Big casually light a tuft of grass and spread the burning pieces around. He panicked and ran to hide in the thickest undergrowth. The merry flames spread in all directions and soon found his place. He screamed and sat still, paralysed by terror. His thin pelt singed off his back and head with a crackle as he hunched there, cooled only by the uncontrolled flow of urine splashing his face.

Big grasped the danger, rushed through the flames, seized Wise Man as easily as if he was a baby and returned to safety. "Don't do that again" he said, brushing ash from his pelt and sniffing the scorched hair on his forearms. He had already realised Wise Man was unlikely to be of practical use, but now he feared he might be a positive liability. On balance he still valued his company enough not to chuck him back in the fire.

Boy and Little became good friends. She was greatly amused by his finicky choice of the tenderest leaf tips, ripest fruit and juiciest grubs. She browsed on everything smaller than a bush and would cheerfully chew right down the stem till her face was buried in soil. She was expert in unearthing bulbs and tubers. She would watch while Boy carefully peeled and washed his share, then doggedly chewed with an expression of pain. Inevitably he would bite on a piece of grit. He would spit and curse and she would cackle with delight.

What pleased her most was to find a bees' nest. The delicious scent of honey had always tantalised Boy, whose apology for a pelt gave no protection from stings. Little had no such problem. Hunched up, covering her face with a broad hand, she would attack the nest with a stout branch. She would prod and prize the hole and withdraw her dripping stave encrusted with wax, honey and crushed larvae. She would then move to the place where Boy waited and share the sweet debris. If the hole was weak enough she would widen it and drag out handfuls of comb, which the whole group could share.

One morning Boy was wandering with her along the broad slope by the river. They were happy. The dewfall was heavy. Fat drops hung from every cobweb and glistened like stars on the tufts of tawny grass. Boy drew in great lungfuls of air and fairly bounded along, kicking up rainbows. It was easy to keep up with Little, who normally was much faster.

"Good morning, beautiful bird" he cried to an ibis. It stared back in astonishment and floated off gracefully through the air. "Hail you fine trees, what lovely fruit you bear! Hail excellent grass, splendid in every way!" Happiness was overflowing into dementia.

The grass opened an eye and growled, twitching its thick-tufted tail. They wasted no time in leaving the tiger to its solitude. Having recently fed, it noted their existence for future reference, rearranged its couch in the long grass and settled down to doze away the day.

The companions sped downriver for two miles. They came to rest at the sunny base of a crumbly cliff. Relief gave extra edge to their delight in being alive.

Boy had noticed a peculiarity in Little. Unlike the tribal females she was never out of season. At his age this was more of a pleasure than a threat. But Wise Man was torn between lust, contempt and incapacity. All the same he felt his seniority required that he enjoy prior rights to Boy, however distasteful the matter might be. Boy disagreed and pushed him over. Little observed their dispute with quiet amusement. Big sensed Wise Man's inadequacy and removed him from contention. He took the struggling elder to the other side of a rock and pacified him by holding a huge fist in front of his nose. The duty of hospitality did not warrant promiscuous gifts to the undeserving.

Boy, thus left alone with his unusual mate, wasted no time in getting to know her. However her weight and strength and her tendency to return his thrusts vigorously, made inadequate the squat posture conventionally adopted by his tribe. He would find himself sent sprawling, or his trembling knees would give out and he would be squashed beneath her. At length, when he was flat on his back for the umpteenth time, Little flopped down beside him and with a brawny arm rolled him upon her chest, as if to suckle him. This position proved satisfactory and they never again deviated from it.

Lying back in a satisfied daze, his eyes idly on a shoal of fleecy clouds, Boy noticed a bee zoom up the cliff and disappear over its rim. Another passed, then another. "Must be a nest up there" he drowsily speculated. Little grunted and yawned. They could have a look later. They dozed for an hour.

The sun's strength roused them by midday. They found the bees' nest in a cleft between a huge rock and a large chunk that had broken away. The size of the smaller piece, deeply embedded in the ground, would have deterred Boy, in spite of his growing strength, but Little did not hesitate. She thrust in her stave and heaved. Bees boiled out in a furious cloud. Boy ran downwind. She put one hand over her muzzle and levered with the other. The rock shifted. It left a splay within which a great mass of honeycomb could be made out.

Boy halted at the top of the cliff. Incautiously he leaned against a sapling. The trunk shuddered and magnified the impulse as it spread, causing a small hornet's nest, which hung at the end of a twig, to dance a vigorous jig. The inhabitants flew out, found Boy and set upon him. He darted off down the cliff like a goat, screaming with pain, swellings appearing all over his body and dived into the first pool he could find.

The hornets patrolled their territory before returning to base and lighted upon Little looking for Boy. Even her pelt could not cope, so she rapidly joined him in the water. They made an incongruous sight, pimpled with stings, furtively rising to the surface for breath, then ducking down again.

Honour satisfied, the hornets returned to their nest. No harm had been done and they cheerfully set about plundering the bees. Boy and Little cautiously left the pool. Their skin and pelt shone glossily in the sun. With groans they kissed and petted each other. Gradually the stings moderated to a general ache. They gingerly reclimbed the cliff and studied the position. Bees and hornets were dangerously numerous all round the nest. If they were to get their hands on the honey, some new strategy was required.

Little hunted among loose rocks and found two sturdy flints. Soon a clump of dry grass was smouldering, and with a puff of breath it burst into flame. She made a bundle of green grass and laid it on the flames. A choking pall rose. She lifted the smouldering mass on two sticks and thrust it in the cleft. The hornets flew away at once and dazed bees crawled out, all fight gone. Little reached into the crevice and withdrew a huge mass of comb.

Boy was intrigued by her magical exploit. Wishing to help, he imitated her actions. He picked a bunch of grass and pushed it into the flames. His bundle, being very dry, instead of smouldering, ignited in a soft explosion and scorched his forearm. He dropped it with an exclamation, the burn intensified by his stings. It fell on a rotten log. Smoke belched and flames enveloped its length in an instant. It had been home to several lizards and a Nile Monitor. They were dead before they thought to escape.

The glowing bark fell away, disclosing the steaming carcasses to Boy, as he stood there licking his burns. He was not one to miss titbits. Little approached with her sweet plunder and crammed a generous handful in his mouth. Unable to speak while he vigorously chewed, he gesticulated at the charred objects. She examined the remains disgustedly. Meat was not part of her menu.

Boy's mouth overflowed. Sugary liquor ran down his chin and onto his chest. Without thinking he rubbed the back of his hand across his mouth. The soreness was immediately soothed by the waxy juice, so he smeared it over his stings and burns. Little did the same. Soon they were both coated in sticky nectar, attracting the attention of ants and flying insects. The friends did not mind, the healing effect was so pleasant.

Boy reached for the first lizard with honey-glazed fingers. He exclaimed at its scorching heat and juggled it from hand to hand, taking tentative bites and spitting it back. The flavour of hot meat and honey was quite different from either, cold and on its own. It was a new dimension. Saliva squirted in his mouth. The moment the lizard leg was cool enough to pass his lips, it was half way to his stomach and he was greedily biting the next.

Little returned to root in the bees' nest. Having finished the lizards, Boy offered her the monitor. But she refused to have anything to do with it. After a few bites, Boy began to feel queasy. He decided Wise Man should have the rest. He was probably still lying in the shade where they had left him, moaning about old age. They made off carrying their winnings on a stretcher of twigs.

"What stupid game is this?" Wise Man had time to wonder as the couple came joyfully to his bivouac. Then the extraordinary scent hit his nostrils, a combination of sweetness and fear. He wrinkled up his nose and sneezed, but at the same time his hands seized the remains of the monitor. "Well, where's the rest?" he demanded as he chewed the last prickly bone. He emitted a belch and at once felt hungry again. Boy shrugged and indicated his own stomach. Wise Man seized his great-nephew's hands and methodically licked all along to his shoulders, not missing an inch. He attempted to give Little the same treatment, but she pushed him away. Big had already cleared the load of honey.

"It isn't good enough. I have to sit here half-starved. All I get is the leavings after you've had your pick. And then you can't be bothered to bring back more than a token. I bet you've got a whole lot more hidden away."

There was no arguing with him. Boy stood up. It was not far back to the bees' nest. Soon they were foraging among the ashes. They found several carbonised grubs, another lizard and a nest of half-grown sizzling mice. Wise Man wept with delight as he ate.

They settled that night in a cave overlooking the river. The meat eaters were inspired to chant the tribal saga. Big and Little covered their ears and clicked disapprovingly. Perhaps, Big thought, it was a mistake to adopt these half-men, they made such tedious sounds.

X

The next day began with a strenuous foray to an uncommonly juicy stand of rushes and sugar cane. The river spread out in an inland delta flanked by fine stands of fever trees, their grey trunks shining in the sun. Big and Little disappeared in the sea of vegetation. Their whereabouts were occasionally disclosed by jerky movements of the reeds, which otherwise tossed their white-flowered heads in unison as the breeze blew.

Boy and Wise Man lay down in the shade to get breath and cool down. Wise Man had the gloomy feeling that all this travel would soon be too much for him. He wondered for the umpteenth time whether he could find his way home to the tribe. If so would they let him stay? He could weep at the thought of the good old roost underfoot. No, it was impossible. His bones were destined to whiten in this desert and his tissues to nourish the scavengers; and, as he presently felt, soon. His stomach rumbled, but he felt too low to forage.

Boy felt no such dejection. He stood up and began to cast about. The shallow pools were coated with mussels and teeming with crabs. He had soon smashed a dozen shellfish open with a pebble and feasted on their succulent flesh. The crabs were more difficult. Their horny, prickly outer parts, once removed, left very little inner tissue. The flavour did not justify the effort and he left the remains for the river birds, which had been following his actions with interest.

With a full belly he drifted off downstream, attracted by the sound of rushing water. Round a bend he found the confluence of his river with another, much larger. Their waters mingled smoothly and poured in a green curving mass down a steep slope, to swish angrily round a large pool, venting thick curds and streaks of foam.

Boy stood stock still, hypnotised by the sight and sound of the standing wave and drowsy from blood concentrating in his belly. He became a creature of the scene, in a trance of awareness for minute after minute.

A chunk of rock clattered down, sending a reflex shock to his toes in one lightning stroke. He leaped in the air and glared up at the source of the noise. A head was visible, peering down. The shock redoubled. It was a person!

Before he knew why, he had emitted a great shout. His body had recognised the newcomer before he had. The cry resolved itself into "Mum!" In a moment they were together. With groans of surprise and joy they studied each other's face, hugged and kissed and danced in a ring. Mum seemed to have shrunk and he mistook Baby for Middle Boy. She could hardly believe that this hulking youth was her weedy eldest son. His scent had changed too. He was mature.

They sat down by the water to chatter and question, interrupting each other as they remembered details, backtracking and repeating themselves. Boy exclaimed with disgust at Mum's expulsion and moaned sympathetically as she displayed her half-healed cuts and bruises. She was shocked at his consorting and mating, with what sounded like a giant baboon, as she unkindly put it. She was amazed that the elder was still alive. She looked forward to giving him a piece of her mind. It was all his fault that things had gone so wrong.

Unexpectedly, her heart melted when she set eyes on Wise Man. How shrunken he was, his head and body hairless, his face wrinkled like a monkey's, his belly sunk from its former rotundity to a flat membrane stretched from ribs to groin. The poor wretch looked half-dead! She fell upon him with the ritual ululation.

"For goodness sake, don't pummel me like that!" Wise Man spat with an invalid's peevishness. All the same, he could not help responding to her much-missed attention. With exaggerated effort, moaning as he struggled up, he embraced her and surprised himself by an upwelling of genuine emotion as they touched. He wept. She wept. They wept together. Middle Boy and Baby joined the chorus. Boy shifted from foot to foot and coughed, avoiding Little's eyes. She and Big looked on with impassive sympathy. Only the twitching of their toes betrayed amusement at this most foreign manifestation.

The reunion went on until late afternoon. Big and Little methodically chewed through the pile of greenery they had gathered. At just the right moment they produced a tiny antelope they had surprised in the reeds. Wise Man speechlessly kissed Big's hands, finger by finger. Mum's eyes almost dropped out, her stomach grumbled and her mouth dripped. Boy came into his own. He kept her off the raw meat, while Big kindled a fire. It was soon flaring briskly on top of the antelope and the scent of charring hair and flesh loaded the thick smoke that swirled about. Mum and the youngsters sprang away the moment they smelt fire, gibbering with terror. Big led them upwind, coughing and spluttering, their eyes full of tears.

The tiger had decided it was time to sample the barefoot prey which had so obligingly intruded on his territory. He had spent over an hour stalking and had arrived within charging range, only to be enveloped by a gout of smoke. It choked his lungs and filled his head with confusion. In hatred and rage he loped away, deep growls rippling his pelt, his mane stiff with fury. The group jumped at the noise, but relaxed once they caught sight of him running over the brow of a distant hill. Their eyes returned to the smouldering deer.

While she waited, Mum thought to take her mind off food by talking to her new friends. She was unsure how much they understood. So, with much smiling and gesticulation, she began. "What a lovely day! Hmmmm... Heap much sun. Cloud done not come. Good eh? Rain, brrrrr.., he done gone long ways."

"It certainly is a splendid day; but it is likely to be cool tonight if there is still no cloud" Big replied without expression.

"If so, we may well have a heavy dewfall" Little added.

Mum could think of no reply. For the first time in her adult life, she was silenced.

Little continued smoothly "As your hide is so poorly covered, it would be advisable to find shelter for the night. There is a comfortable cave quite nearby. Once you have eaten, I suggest we go there. We shall need to collect more supplies on the way, as there are now seven to feed."

"Mum! The food is ready." Boy was waving a blackened foreleg by the hoof. As soon as the meat had cooled enough Mum and Middle Boy tore it apart. Wise Man and Baby squabbled over another leg. Showing no respect for his senior, Baby snatched the steaming joint and sprinted away to devour it. Boy handed another chunk of meat to the furious elder, who sat down, still grumbling about Baby's rudeness. Mum would have rebuked them both, if she were not in a paradise of roast meat. As it was, silence fell while the family ate.

Boy raked the embers away and turned the shrunken remains. The antelope's blood and juices had settled and soaked into the soil, forming a mud mould, which cracked off with the hide as he rolled it. The whole flank was tender and moist, far tastier than the lizards. It only needed sweetening to be perfect.

Big and Little moved away from the offensive smell of burnt meat and started talking. Their limbs waved gracefully as they conversed, each syllable's multiple meaning being shaped as appropriate by the gesture of a crooked toe, a tone, or by a particular odour and in most cases by all three. Their discussion dealt with the future of their guests. It lasted ten seconds, such was the compactness of their language.

They decided that, out of common decency, they could not abandon these ill-prepared creatures to the unforgiving savannah and its residents. It would be hard to provide for such a large group, but Big thought Wise Man would soon be carrion. The three young males stood a chance of adapting if they had time to learn. Mum deserved special protection as the only female. Little hoped Wise Man would be able to breed from her before it was too late. By a mild gesture of uncertainty she conveyed that she was herself feeling unwell, putting it down to the poisonous fumes off the antelope.

The company lay down for a short siesta while their meal settled.

XI

The cave was a huge sandstone overhang, approached by a narrow path zig-zagging up the river cliff. This opened into a broad shelf at the base of the overhang. It was a favourite haunt of rock swallows, whose twitters and swerving flight peopled the air throughout the day. At sunset millions of bats would emerge from deep recesses where they hung, so well camouflaged that only restive twitches, a drizzle of droppings and shrill squabbles betrayed their presence. A slight trickle of water from the underlip of the overhang had hollowed a little pool in front of the cave. The excess trickled over the shelf and formed a damp patch on the wall of the gorge. Even in the driest of dry seasons, when the river sank to a disconnected series of mudholes and stagnant pools, it persisted, drops falling at intervals with a crisp echo.

Vines and flowering creepers covered the ends of the cave, climbing over each other half way to the roof and stretching out along the cliff. The fruiting season was not yet over. Baby and Middle Boy enjoyed themselves, clambering along the precarious stems to where the juiciest grapes swung. The steep rock face was as easy for them as for monkeys. Boy took responsibility for the stores. He carefully placed the bunches in the pool to keep them clean and cool.

Their new refuge could hardly have been safer. Its only defect was the lack of escape route should an enemy mount the steep path.

It took a while for the group to settle to its new way of life. At times Big found the continuous chatter of people almost unbearable. Why did they have to keep repeating the obvious? But Little took to the children so well that Boy felt quite jealous. Mum felt shy and unsure of herself. She had at last met someone whose verbal powers outmatched hers, so she chattered nervously whenever she was with Big. It was like being an immature girl all over again. He kept a watchful eye on her as they foraged. When she came back into season Wise Man was called into service. It was not very satisfactory - he could hardly muster the energy to stand properly to her. Old age was claiming him, he moaned, with rheumy half-shut eyes.

The dry season ended in a terrible thunderstorm. They cowered in the cave for three days while wind and rain did their worst. The river became a torrent reaching halfway up the cliff, their trickling waterfall turned into a splashing sheet across the cave mouth and the walls sweated. Their bedding fermented and stank. Big and Little consumed it with every sign of pleasure and became unreasonably merry. They danced and tumbled, carefree as the swallows that watched from above with beady eyes.

The people sat disconsolate and unamused, shifting about irritably to avoid the revellers and drops of water from the roof. Wise Man's joints creaked and ached in the damp. He felt that he would never again swing through the treetops. It would be bad enough getting from place to place on the ground.

Mum came into season again at this time, adding to Wise Man's sense of impotence. Wearily he stood to her again. Things were soon over. Big helped him away to rest and returned to Mum to cheer her up.

The ground dwellers' pelts laughed off both rain and heat. An undercoat grew in the wet season, making them even bulkier. It was this that disguised Little's condition, from herself as well as Big and made her birth pangs such a surprise. It was her first parturition, so she had no idea what to expect. She ejected a moist bundle on the sandy floor. "It's bald!" she groaned, giving Boy an accusing look. This was not strictly true. The pup was covered in a slick coat of lanugo so short and shiny with moisture that it looked like skin.

Big cupped the object in one massive palm and examined it minutely. "It isn't like any normal child. It's female, but it has only two nipples! And what a huge head!" He studied the tiny creature with a look of complete amazement. After a moment he added "I never dreamed that you and Boy could be fertile. Congratulations... Dad!" He seized Boy's hand with a ferocious smile and placed it in his mouth. His jaws closed firmly, but only hard enough to bruise the knuckles without breaking the skin.

Little produced three more pups in rapid succession, all female. Boy was appalled. He hid in the back of the cave. He felt unreasonably guilty, as if he had taken advantage of Big, as Wise Man had cheated Dad. Would Big treat him in the same way? Anyway, he felt far too immature to accept the responsibility conveyed by these strange hybrids. All the same there was no denying that he was now Dad.

Mum was equally unready to be Gran, but she could not help wanting to touch and fondle these unexpected new members of the family. She approached as Little was biting off the cords and gently took the first in her arms. She cuddled it and kissed its creased face. It immediately gave a loud angry cry, not unlike the mew of a tiger cub. The others joined in, adding a new counterpoint to the echoes of the cave. Little snatched her baby back with a possessive glare. She was very nervous of these unknowns and not sure whether they were worth preserving, but she wasn't going to let Gran damage them.

The babies certainly showed little promise. Their birth hair fell out in a few days, leaving them completely bald. They lacked the instinct to clutch their mother's pelt, nor could they walk. They cried for trifling reasons, alerting predators, and could only be pacified by immediate feeding. Although Little had sufficient nipples, it was a difficult trick to hold all four at the same time. Likewise, they had to be carried everywhere, a danger and a nuisance, especially as they grew very rapidly. Gran and Dad helped lug them about, but they both felt the strain, tiring surprisingly quickly. Every time they went foraging they were vulnerable.

It occurred to Big that the only solution was to divide the work. He and Dad went out with the lads, while the females and Wise Man, now a demoralised drone, minded the children. This was unpopular with Gran and Little who soon became bored. A compromise was finally decided. The duties were alternated, though, before weaning, Little had to get back sooner than she wished to feed the babies.

The reason for Gran's weakness soon became obvious. She too was pregnant. Wise Man was not quite the crock he seemed. The news changed him overnight. He swelled visibly, ate for two and it was not long before his paunch rivalled hers. He strutted about as if he owned the place.

The thin pelt regrew along his back and limbs, but not on his head. He even began to search for food again.

As Boy was now Dad his brothers each moved up a notch in the pecking order. Marks of full maturity appeared on Dad, a gingery goatee, shaggy eyebrows and a rolling gait to emphasise the weight of his testicles. The youths showed scant respect. They often could be seen imitating his tread with much sniggering and dodging out of reach as he tried to cuff them. They could always escape by scuttling up the cave wall. They would rest on some tiny ledge and pelt him with bird dung and pieces of nests. New Boy even pissed on his head once, as he stood below cursing.

The wet season ended. It was the easy feeding season, when food could be found on every bush. The babies grew fast. A pelt appeared at last, but only on their heads. This was fortunate as they began to toddle about the cave and were soon covered in bruises and cuts. Their hair protected their heads from some damage. But they showed no natural caution and were slow to learn. One walked off the edge of the cliff and was killed. She was buried under a pile of rocks at the back of the cliff.

This event cast a strange light on the baby Gran bore with great hardship soon after. There was always the vague impression that it was partly Little's, even though it was a large boy and much more normal-looking than the girls, with a luxuriant coat, deep-set wise eyes and all the proper instincts. He could hop onto Gran's back within an hour and would hang on with the strength of a hyaena's jaws even when asleep. This made foraging a little easier, but his weight increased rapidly, as he helped himself from Little as well as from Gran. Little was happy to oblige, as the girls consumed only half her lactation. Soon he would run alongside Gran, or ride on Little, as Gran's back was not strong enough for his weight.

Not long after Gran's confinement, Big disappeared without a word. He was not to be found anywhere. Little surmised that he was off to the mountains in search of a new mate. She would miss him - no more sensible conversations until he got back. Her thoughts broke off as she rushed to rescue one of the children which had just tumbled in the pool.

Big did not return. Wise Man supposed the tiger had caught him. Gran kicked him when he said this. Little refused to speculate. Soon he was unthought of.

The girls showed no sign of Boy's fear of heights. At the time of ripe fruit and nuts they learned the art of climbing. Soon they were clambering about the bushes to knock down the next meal. Accidents happened. One fell on her head. She was silly the rest of her life, though this did not prevent her from having five children. Another endured a crooked arm. The third grew up without accidental damage, but she and her sisters could never learn more than a smattering of Little's language, being physically much more like Dad, and lacking the rich repertoire of scent and vocalisation of the ground-dwellers.

XII

One morning, not unlike the time when the family had been reunited, Boy was foraging with his younger brother. He was as tall as Dad and showed signs of maturity, bad temper, restlessness and a hunger unsatisfied however many insects and shoots he crammed in his mouth. He could hardly wait for the girls to grow up, he grumbled to himself, as they went along. His brother said helpfully "Why don't you have a talk with Little? She is such a sweetie. She'll know what to do."

Boy blushed at the idea. "Come on. Toss me off" he pleaded offering his inflamed penis as if it were some choice morsel.

"Get stuffed!" His brother scampered half way up the cliff to a rock dove's nest. He seized a squab, stuffed it in his mouth and threw its sibling down to Boy. It hit him in the face. In the scuffle that ensued they both failed to notice the advent of a bear. It stopped a few feet from them and appraised the kicks, cuffs and wrestling holds employed, with an expert eye. As it was leaning against the cliff when they noticed it, they could not escape by climbing. Instead they took to their heels towards the cave. Foolishly they did not run in different directions, so the bear did not have to choose between them. It lolloped behind at an easy gallop, deceptively so, with its enormous bulk, closing by the second.

They reached the cliff path just ahead of the bear. The rest of the group was at home and the boys' terrified yells brought a line of spectators to the cliff edge. The younger lad was quicker on a slope than his brother, so the bear tripped the latter by the heel and gathered him up. He was soon silent, but his horror-struck relatives made up for that. They even hurled down rocks upon the bear's well-padded back and neck as it chewed and mangled its prey. Irritated, it removed the carcass to a quieter, shady spot down river. Soon nothing remained to evidence Boy's existence. The bear shambled away to sleep off her meal.

The family, subdued, fearful and grief-stricken, prepared for the night. Heartbroken as she was, Gran was not the sort to fail to mark such an event. She began a long defiant panegyric in memory of Boy, bayed at the impartial sky. Soon the rest of the family picked up on it and joined the chorus. Little added an accompaniment, slapping her reverberant belly and banging a pebble on the ground. The babies added their wails and Wise Man leaped up. Forgetting his aches he performed an impromptu dance, his whole body expressing the pain and brevity of life, tossed like a leaf in the wind from event to accident. It ended abruptly when he stumbled into the pool and not only got wet but sprained an ankle. His shrill cries of pain, diminishing to whimpers, made a perfect finale.

For many days afterwards the group took care to minimise the hazards of foraging, going out en masse, and a sentry always kept watch while the rest searched. The yield of fruit and nuts was heavy and the cave became littered with piles of provisions. Little had a rick of greenery. The pool overflowed with grapes, pomegranates, figs and hands of bananas.

With all this food the babies grew very rapidly. Little's three were as big as Dad had been after two years. Gran's new boy became stranger by the day. He grew, as it were, from the shoulders downwards. His arms lengthened fast. Soon they reached further than his toes and he would rest his hands with bent elbows upon the backs of his broad feet. He walked in a stiff posture, his whole body swinging from left to right and right to left, carried forward by his stilt-like arms. He looked like a mobile coconut whose rind had ripened and frayed, with his topknot of unruly ginger hair. Gran was unreasonably proud of him. Wise Man was not. Although the child showed a quick grasp of language and even made amazing progress with Little's tongue, there was no physical trace of Wise Man's physique. It took him a long time to suspect the truth, mainly because he could not face it.

At the time concerned, no name had yet been given to Gran's boy. It was normal to wait a while in case the infant died. If this happened the name might haunt the group, seeking its envelope, disturbing their dreams and jinxing their days, until a new child came, to which it could be attached. Later deaths, such as Boy's, were still worse because they altered the group's structure. But by then name and body were so attached that they expired together, leaving no echoes of half-existence.

Gran thought it was high time her boy was given a name and as he was so unusual, this should be allowed for. Little's children were already possessors of names which they would never be able to pronounce. In the language of the tribe they were called Thumb, Forefinger and Middle Finger. But Little Finger was not at all suitable for Gran's boy. She raised the matter with Wise Man as they rooted in a marsh for bulbs.

Wise Man squatted in the cooling mud, resting his hands below the surface. His eyes travelled to the spot where the child was turning over pebbles and cramming worms in his mouth. His agility, his rapid scuttles from stone to stone, the swift pounce upon his wriggling prey, all revolted Wise Man. The brat did not evoke the slightest affection. This of course was a father's normal reaction to a son who might threaten him when he grew up. But the thatch of hair, the deformed legs and those extraordinary arms, the deep-sunk eyes... If he did not know better, he would have thought it was a child of Big!

The thought had no sooner occurred than it possessed him. He felt an irresistible tremor run through his brain, turning memory upside down and inside out. Of course. His mouth was full of bitter saliva. So kind of Big to help him out of sight! He stood up and waded to the nearest tree. A handy stick was available. With a scream he landed a heavy blow on Gran's back.

She took it. The rotten wood broke as it landed and did no more than bruise. She turned her face to his and looked, a knowing, gentle stare. He froze in fighting pose. His eyes failed before her. His shoulders sagged. His legs gave way. He slumped in the mud.

"I am sorry. You are too old." She took him by the ears, drew his face to her and kissed his bald forehead. Tears ran down both their faces.

Wise Man could bear no more. He rose, heart aching, every bone creaking and spoke. "I have no right to name him." He turned away and slowly headed back to the cave to shade his misery. The rest of the group followed.

The tiger had by no means given up hope of tasting the people. He too was elderly and his worn teeth could hardly cope with the tough hide of his usual prey. This was assuming he could catch anything, an open question these days. A short sprint or a single leap was possible, though he paid the penalty of aching muscles and jarred joints afterwards. His coat had lost its gloss, his mane was falling out, and his tail tuft dragged in the dust. He suffered from intestinal parasites, angina and permanent diarrhoea, and one eye had been badly scratched by a thorn. He could only see blurred shapes with it. He had failed to find a mate again that year.

He had studied the people with care. He had a horror of crowds and their habit of foraging in groups made him unwilling to risk an attack. All the same he did not give up hope of catching a straggler. He would lie up the far side of the valley, concealed in rocks and watch them come and go. At other times he sprawled on the plateau above the cave and listened indulgently to the racket that rose from below.

The last day had been bad. He had missed an easy kill - a pregnant antelope. Landing, he sprained a paw. The shock upset his system and he was gripped by another bout of diarrhoea. He felt too weak to hunt and staggered to ground across the valley from the cave.

Gradually the cramps in his belly subsided and he slept. When he woke his mind was crystal clear. "Food or death" was his only thought. He peered about with his good eye. The squall of brats and Dad's angry shouts came to him. Wise Man limped glumly to the edge to urinate. He looked exactly what the tiger needed, plump, with plenty of marrow-bones, and very vulnerable. The elder plodded back out of sight.

The moment he rose, weakness put its foot on the tiger's back. He dragged himself, as if he was carrying a buffalo, wearily across the valley. He took three rests behind bushes on the way before he reached the foot of the cliff. It was fortunate the group was too busy among itself to remember to post a look-out. The cliff path looked insuperable, but once he had placed a paw on it, the delicious spoor overwhelmed his weariness. His limbs moved as if they belonged to a different beast. He mounted at a pace that would not have disgraced his prime, crouched in the proper way and cautiously peeped over the lip.

Dad was at that moment trying to break up a fight between his brother, Big's boy and his children. As in most family squabbles, the cause was too trivial and complicated to be established, but as a result, the fighting was that much more bitter. The tiger was thus almost able to join the family before it was noticed.

Wise Man stood dejectedly out of harm's way by the pool. He had just helped himself to a fig and was chewing this as he miserably considered his position. He was so preoccupied that it took a moment for the furry boulder rising on the path to register. He made up for his initial slowness by a simultaneous scream and amazing leap that carried him right past the combatants, followed by a sprint which did not cease until he was hanging by his hands from a ledge twenty feet up the cave wall. The whole group froze and followed him with their eyes. They had never seen him move so fast.

By now the tiger's spurt of energy had run out, so when their eyes returned to the cave mouth, he was in the process of slumping down beside the pool. Even so he made a formidable sight, fully justifying employment in the tribe's most damning curse. The group wasted no time. They joined Wise Man as high up the cave wall as each member could climb.

The tiger's mouth hung half-open, great gasps rattling his lolling tongue. He could make out his prey hanging in the dim shade like fruit ready for plucking. There was no escape and so, no hurry, he realised with pleasure. The sweetish smell of fermenting juice caught his attention. He was even thirstier than he was hungry. He tried to move. A deep groan was the only result. It chilled his listener's hearts. A stern effort brought his muzzle to the pool. His eyes closed. He began a steady lapping. Soon he was purring contentedly. He felt an influx of power warming every part of his body. At last he stopped and gave a mighty yawn. The smell of his breath drifted through the cave, poisoning the air. Dad gagged and sneezed.

The tiger opened its eyes. They disclosed only confusing shadows. He shut the bad eye and concentrated on the good one. Now he could make out the cave walls, but they seemed to be moving, almost toppling. He felt dizzy. He shut his eye again. The feeling got worse, as if he was sliding over the cliff and at the same time the cave was spinning round him. Bewildered and giddy he let out a grumbling roar. It was better to open his eyes. The world steadied.

Gran and Little were far from happy with the situation. They had settled on a narrow and uncomfortable ledge, their children, still bickering, nearby. They took hold of some rocks and lobbed them at the tiger. The rest of the group joined in and soon a hailstorm was pelting him. Little's long arms gave extra force to her shots. One particularly well-aimed rock hit an eyetooth and snapped it off. The tiger was well-acquainted with pain, but, combined with humiliation, it reached new levels of anguish. He stood up with a roar, shaking with fury and weaving vertiginously.

At this point Wise Man's inadequate hold failed. He tumbled lithely down, coming to rest a few feet from the tiger. He was on the side of the bad eye, so instead of immediately pouncing, the tiger turned his head for a better view. He moved with drunken caution and while he did, Wise Man sprinted for the cave mouth. His enemy sprang after him, but so clumsily that he fell over.

Gamely he rose and, placing each paw with exaggerated caution in the right spot, followed the elder, who by now was half out of sight down the path. As the tiger went, his coordination improved and he accelerated. In a few seconds he was with his prey and offered a blow. Wise Man saw it and leaped clear. This was the end. He left the path and flew down the face of the cliff. The rocky river bed terminated his shriek.

To run down a steep twisting cliff path on three legs whilst both drunk and unwell proved impossible. The tiger's feet tangled, tripped him and he too was airborne before Wise Man was half-way down. He impacted within a yard of the deceased elder. After a feeble twitch or two, life departed.

The group descended from the cave and examined the broken bodies with respective horror and delight. Dad had Wise Man's corpse carried up and buried honourably at the back of the cave. They ate the tiger.

As long as grapes and other fruit were available, the pool was stocked. It served to rinse the fruit, as the source of many happy drunken evenings and as a last line of defence. It was named Wise Man's Pool after the heroic elder who saved the tribe at its very beginning.

Mum, Little and Dad left no memorial, only a new race. But that is another story.